Submarines

Heather Hammonds

Chapter 1

Submarines

Many ships travel across the seas of the world. Some are big and some are small. All of them float on top of the sea.

Submarines are water craft that can travel under the sea, as well as on top of it.

Submarines can dive deep under the sea. Submarine **crews** stay safe inside their craft, as they travel beneath the waves.

When they are underwater, submarines cannot be seen by ships or aeroplanes.

Some submarines can dive more than 250 metres underwater. That's a long way down!

3

In many countries, submarines are owned by the **navy**. The navy uses submarines to:

- help **protect** the country they belong to

- help protect ships travelling from country to country

- learn more about the seas of the world.

How a Submarine Rises and Sinks

A submarine floats, just like a ship.

To make a submarine go under the sea, tanks inside it are filled with water.

To make a submarine go up, air is pushed into the tanks. Water is pushed out by the air.

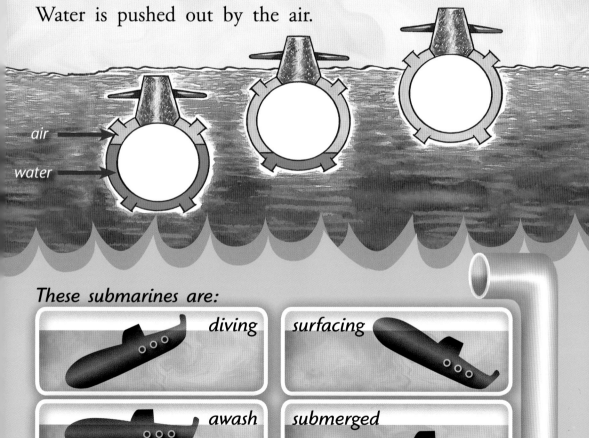

air

water

These submarines are:

diving

surfacing

awash

submerged

Chapter 2

The First Submarines

The first submarines were built hundreds of years ago.

To travel underwater, people needed:

- air, to breathe

- a way to make submarines move through the water

- a way to make submarines go up and down in the water.

The first submarine was built in England, in 1626.

It was rowed along by twelve men. Special tubes let air into the submarine for people to breathe.

The first submarines could not stay underwater for very long.

A submarine called the Turtle was built in 1776. The Turtle was made from wood and metal. It was shaped a little bit like an egg!

Propellers pushed the Turtle through the water. A person inside pushed pedals to make the propellers go around.

The First Metal Submarine

The first metal submarine was built in 1800. It was called the Nautilus. A propeller pushed it along when it was underwater. It also had a big sail, like a ship's.

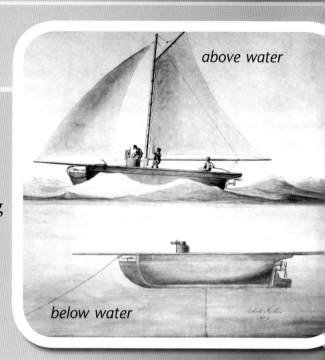

above water

below water

Today, submarines have propellers that are turned by big engines.

9

Modern Submarines

This submarine uses diesel fuel.

Today's submarines are much faster and quieter than submarines of the past.

Some submarines use batteries and **diesel fuel** to make them go.

Other submarines use **nuclear power** to make them go.

Submarines do not have windows. It is very dark under the sea, so windows are not needed.

Computers and other special machines are used to help steer submarines.

Submarines also have a **periscope** so that people inside the submarine can see above the water.

Air and Water ⊙⊙⊙⊙⊙⊙

Modern submarines can stay underwater for a long time. Machines on the submarines make air to breathe. Drinking water is made from salty sea water.

This crew has air to breathe and water to drink.

Hide and Seek

Submarines can travel very quietly underwater. Their engines make very little noise.

It is hard for ships and other submarines to find them.

Sonar is used on submarines, so the crew can listen to sounds around them.

Submarines are painted black. This makes them hard to see.

Chapter 4

Submariners

People who work on submarines are called submariners.

Submariners do jobs such as:

- working on radios
- working on computers
- working on the submarine's engines
- cooking food for other members of the crew.

There are lots of different jobs on submarines!

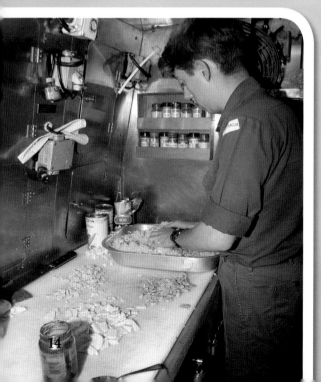

Smaller submarines have crews of around 50 people. Bigger submarines have crews of more than 100 people.

It is very crowded, even on the biggest submarines.

Each submarine has a Commanding Officer. The Commanding Officer is in charge of the submarine.

To: Zac@navybase.com
From: Tess@pinet.com

Dear Uncle Zac,

Do you like your new job as a submariner?

What do you do?

What are the best and worst things about your job?

Tess

Submariners get emails from friends and family when they are not at sea, in their submarines. They are not allowed to send or receive emails from the submarines.

Dear Tess,

I love being a submariner!

I work on the submarine's engines. When I am not working, I sleep and eat my meals.

I do exercises to keep fit. I also do extra study to learn more about my job. The best thing about my job is that it is very exciting. The worst thing about my job is that I am away from home for so long.

Uncle Zac

Four meals a day are served on board submarines. Breakfast, lunch, dinner and a midnight meal are served.

17

Chapter 5

Submarine Accidents

Sometimes submarine accidents happen. Water may get inside a submarine if there is an accident.

However, today's submarines are safer than ever before. Submarine accidents do not happen very often.

The crew on a submarine often have training exercises. This prepares them for any accidents that may occur.

*A Deep **Submersible** Rescue Vehicle*

Submarines have **escape towers**, in case they sink. The crew of the submarine wear special suits when they use the escape towers.

Small rescue submarines are also used to help submariners escape.

Chapter 6

Exploring the Deep

Some small kinds of submarine are used to study the deepest parts of the sea. They are called submersibles.

Submersibles do not stay under the sea for as long as bigger submarines. But they can dive much deeper.

Submersibles have helped scientists learn about:

- animals that live deep under the sea

- volcanoes under the sea

- ships that have sunk.

This submersible can dive 4 500 metres beneath the sea!

Chapter 7

Future Submarines

Submarines have changed a lot since the first wooden submarines.

What will submarines of the future be like?

Submarines of the future will be even faster than today's submarines.

They may look very different.

Submarines of the future will be even quieter than today's submarines. It will be harder for ships and other submarines to find them.

Maybe one day you will join the navy and travel on a submarine!

Countries around the world keep their new submarine ideas secret, so other countries do not build them first.

Glossary

crews	groups of people who work together on a submarine or a ship
diesel fuel	a type of fuel used to run trucks, ships and some other machines
escape towers	towers inside submarines that are used to escape from, if a submarine sinks
navy	a group of people and water craft that patrol the sea and protect the country they belong to
nuclear power	a kind of power that makes heat, which is used to run machines and make electricity
periscope	a long tube that lets people inside a submarine see above the water
propellers	blades on the back of water craft that help push them through the water
protect	look after, and keep safe from harm
sonar	sonar stands for SOund Navigation And Ranging. It is an instrument that uses sound to find out where things are underwater.
submersibles	small submarines that can dive very deep and are used to study the deepest parts of the sea

Index

24